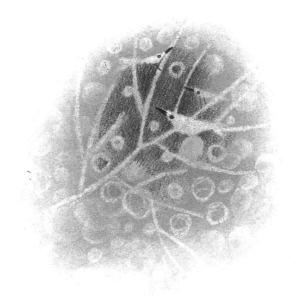

THE
SOUR CHERRY
TREE

For my brother Neil.
Thank you for always
remembering.

— N.H.

To the memory of
my grandfather, who
was my first and best
storyteller.

— N.K.

THE
SOUR CHERRY
TREE

Written by
NASEEM HRAB

Illustrated by
NAHID KAZEMI

OWLKIDS BOOKS

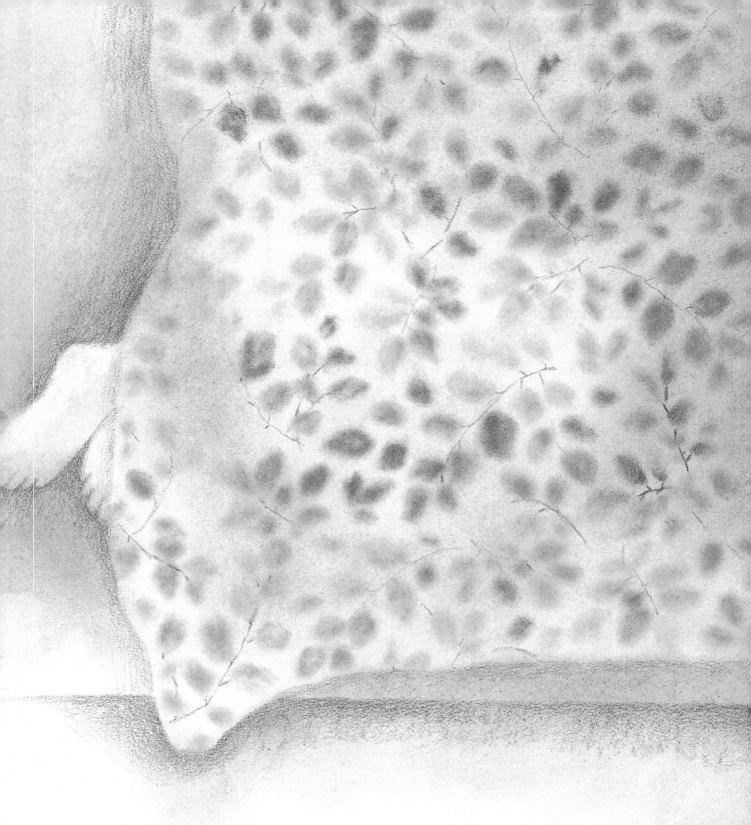

I BIT MY MOM ON THE TOE THIS MORNING.

Not too hard. Just hard enough to wake her.

My baba bozorg forgot to wake up yesterday. He lived alone, so no one was there to bite him.

I really wish I'd been there.

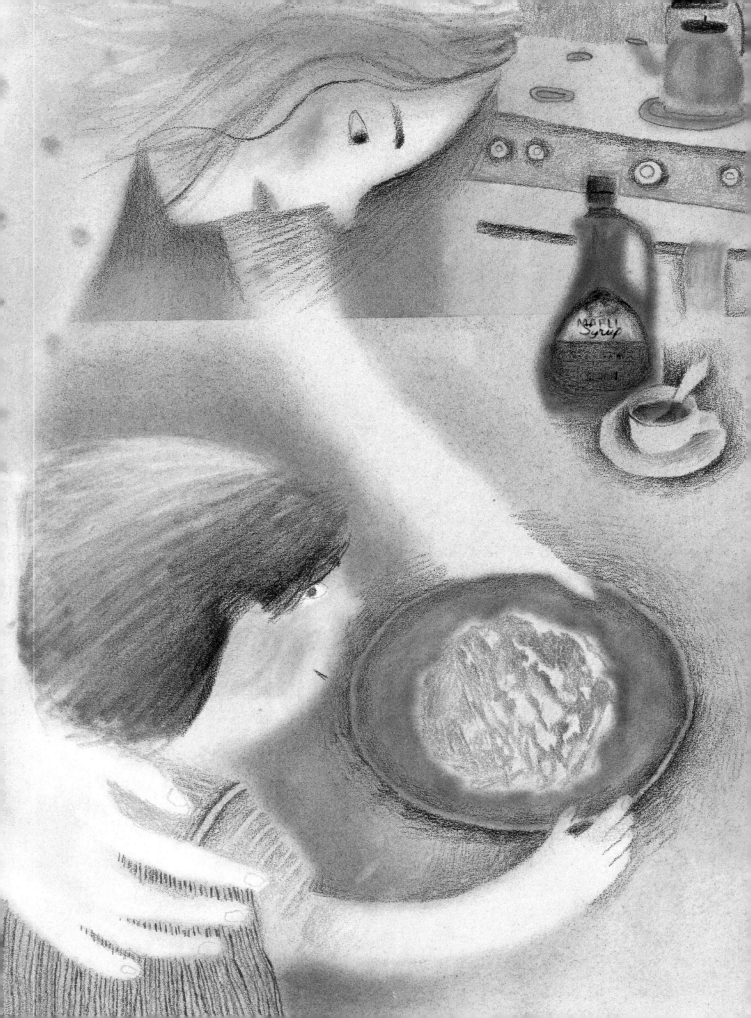

My mom made pancakes with maple syrup for
breakfast, but I don't feel like eating them.

I give my pancake a kiss on each cheek. It looks
like my baba bozorg.

It has his ears.

Mom frowns. "Don't play with your food," she says.

"But it looks like Baba-joon!" I say. "See?"

Mom looks. Then she laughs and kisses my
pancake on the forehead.

After breakfast, we go to Baba Bozorg's house.
"To take care of a few things," says Mom.

Sometimes, Baba Bozorg was napping when we visited him. We could hear his snores from the hallway. Mom would tell me to jump on his bed to wake him up.

I walk up the stairs to his bedroom and look inside.

There's a crumpled-up tissue on his nightstand.
Smudgy eyeglasses. A picture of my mom and
Baba Bozorg standing under the sour cherry
tree. The tree looks small, and so does my mom.

I get up on his bed, jump once, and get down.
It's not the same.

Baba Bozorg's slippers rest on the rug. I put them on and
shuffle to his closet.

He always kept mints in his pockets. I check all his shirts
and pants but only find wrappers.

I try to walk down the stairs in his slippers, but it's too hard. So I sit down and take them off.

I can hear Mom talking on the phone.

"No, no funeral. He didn't want us to make a fuss," she says. "He just wanted us all to eat lunch at Sunshine's."

"Can I order chicken fingers?" I call as I carry the slippers downstairs. I love plum sauce.

Baba Bozorg's favorite teacup is sitting on the kitchen counter next to his samovar. He liked hot Ceylon tea with a splash of rose water and a fig cookie.

I don't really like fig cookies. But he always gave me one, and I always took one because we didn't share many words.

I shuffle into the living room and slip behind the curtains. This was Baba Bozorg's favorite hiding spot. I could always see his slippers peeking out, but I pretended that I couldn't.

When I finally found him, he would say, "Many good!"

I liked the way he said words.

There's a basket of my mom's old toys behind the curtains. I would play with them while Baba Bozorg and Mom talked. Baba Bozorg spoke Farsi loudly but English quietly.

I don't speak Farsi loudly or quietly, so I would just listen for my name. Baba Bozorg gave me a wink whenever I caught them.

His eyebrows were as long as a cat's whiskers.

I fly an airplane into the study.

Baba Bozorg was a poet in Iran. I open one of his notebooks and flip through each page. His words look like squiggles and dots to me.

Maybe Mom knows what they mean.

I go outside. I look up at the house. I can feel
the sun on my cheeks.

I walk under the sour cherry tree and crush
the cherries on the sidewalk with my feet.

One by one.

Mom comes outside and stands beside me.
 "I was your age when he planted it," she says.
 I touch the tree trunk with my hand. The
leaves rustle in the wind.

Whenever we left Baba Bozorg's house, he would wave at us until I couldn't see him anymore.

Owlkids Books acknowledges the financial support of the Canada Council for the Arts, the Ontario Arts Council, the Government of Canada through the Canada Book Fund (CBF) and the Government of Ontario through the Ontario Creates Book Initiative for our publishing activities.

Published in Canada by Owlkids Books Inc., 1 Eglinton Avenue East, Toronto, ON M4P 3A1

Published in the US by Owlkids Books Inc., 1700 Fourth Street, Berkeley, CA 94710

Library of Congress Control Number: 2020951531

Library and Archives Canada Cataloguing in Publication

Title: The sour cherry tree / written by Naseem Hrab ; illustrated by Nahid Kazemi.
Names: Hrab, Naseem, author. | Kazemi, Nahid, illustrator.
Identifiers: Canadiana 20200409816 | ISBN 9781771474146 (hardcover)
Classification: LCC PS8615.R317 S68 2021 | DDC jC813/.6—dc23

Edited by Karen Li and Karen Boersma | Designed by Alisa Baldwin

Manufactured in Shenzhen, Guangdong, China, in May 2021, by WKT Co. Ltd.
Job #20CB2366

A   B   C   D   E   F

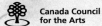

Publisher of Chirp, Chickadee and OWL
www.owlkidsbooks.com

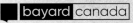
Owlkids Books is a division of bayard canada